ABOUT BABA YAGA

Baba Yaga is one of the most important figures in Russian folklore. She appears, in one form or another, in hundreds of folktales. Sometimes she is the fearsome witch, as in this story, but sometimes she is kind and even helpful. She is so familiar to Russian children that she's almost a member of the family—like an elderly aunt who is either mean or nice, depending on her mood.

Baba Yaga lives deep in the darkest woods of Russia, in a small hut that has chicken legs and that turns around at her command. She flies over the countryside in a mortar and pestle. In some stories she has children, servants, a big black cat, a fierce dog, and flocks of wild geese. Sometimes she eats her children (by mistake, of course), but they always reappear in the next story.

The text of this book is based primarily on a story called "Tereshichka," which I translated and retold from the Russian folktales collected by Aleksandr Afanas'ev and published in serial form from 1855 to 1864. Tereshichka is the name of the young boy, but I have changed to it "Tishka" to make it easier to pronounce.

The style I've used for the illustrations was inspired by "lubok" pictures, a type of Russian folk art that first appeared in the 17th century. The earliest lubok pictures were hand-colored woodcuts. They combined words and pictures (often in several panels) to tell a religious story, a historical incident, a political satire, or a folktale. The crude, simple shapes and bold coloring of lubok pictures perfectly match the mood and period of the Baba Yaga stories.

—K.A.

To Marjorie Nathanson, Jill Ciment, and Vladimir Radunsky, who encouraged me and helped to get me started.
The art for this book was prepared first as black line drawings. These were used as guidelines for the full-color art, which was painted with gouache on watercolor paper. The line drawings were then photographed separately for greater contrast and sharpness. Copyright © 1993 by Katya Arnold. All rights reserved. No part of this book may be reproduced or utilized in any form or by any means, electronic or mechanical, including photocopying, recording, or any information storage and retrieval system, without permission in writing from the publisher. Published in the United States by North-South Books Inc., New York. Published simultaneously in Great Britain, Canada, Australia, and New Zealand by North-South Books, an imprint of Nord-Süd Verlag AG, Gossau Zürich, Switzerland. Designed by Marc Cheshire.

Library of Congress Cataloging-in Publication Data
Arnold, Katya.
Baba Yaga: a Russian folktale / retold and illustrated by Katya Arnold.
Summary: The witch Baba Yaga uses a trick to capture a young man, but he cleverly avoids being eaten.
1. Baba Yaga (Legendary character)—Legends. [1. Baba Yaga (legendary character)
2. Fairy tales. 3. Folklore—Russia.] I. Title.
PZ8.A868Bab 1993 398.22—dc20
[E] 92-38199

British Library Cataloguing in Publication Data
Baba Yaga: Russian Folk Tale
I. Arnold, Katya
823

ISBN 1-55858-208-8 (trade binding) 10 9 8 7 6 5 4 3 2 1
ISBN 1-55858-209-6 (library binding) 10 9 8 7 6 5 4 3 2 1
ISBN 1-55858-593-1 (paperback) 10 9 8 7 6 5 4 3 2 1
Printed in Belgium

BABA YAGA

A RUSSIAN FOLKTALE

RETOLD AND ILLUSTRATED BY
KATYA ARNOLD

NORTH-SOUTH BOOKS / NEW YORK

ONCE upon a time there lived an old man and an old woman. They had been married for fifty years but had no children to brighten their old age, no one to bring them a cup of tea or chop the wood for the fire, no one to care for them when they got frail. This made them very sad.

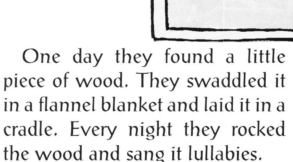

One day they found a little piece of wood. They swaddled it in a flannel blanket and laid it in a cradle. Every night they rocked the wood and sang it lullabies.

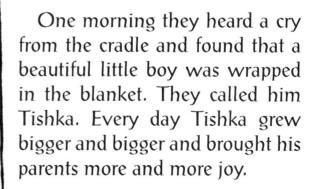

One morning they heard a cry from the cradle and found that a beautiful little boy was wrapped in the blanket. They called him Tishka. Every day Tishka grew bigger and bigger and brought his parents more and more joy.

When Tishka was old enough, his father built him a little rowboat for fishing. Every morning Tishka fished, and every afternoon his mother stood on the shore of the lake and called: "Tishka, Tishka, bread and meat. Come ashore, it's time to eat!" Tishka would row to shore, and while he ate, his mother would carry his fish home.

One day Tishka's mother warned him about Baba Yaga, a wicked witch who lived nearby. Baba Yaga was feared by everyone because she snatched up little children and ate them. "So, my little Tishka dear, never, never let her near!"

The second his mother went away, Baba Yaga appeared on the shore and called out in her screeching voice: "Tishka, Tishka, bread and meat. Come ashore, it's time to eat!"

Tishka was very young, but he was clever. So he yelled back: "That's not my mother's voice I hear. I think that Baba Yaga's near."

When she heard this, Baba Yaga grew furious. She ran to the blacksmith and asked him to cast her a thin metal tongue so her voice would sound as melodious as Tishka's mother's.

Then back to the shore she went and called out in her new singsong voice: "Tishka, Tishka, bread and meat. Come ashore, it's time to eat!"

This time Tishka came ashore. Baba Yaga jumped out from behind a tree, grabbed Tishka, and stuffed him into a dirty canvas sack.

Then she ran through the forest until she got to her hut. The hut spun around on its chicken legs and the front door popped open.

Hoisting the canvas sack up the ladder, Baba Yaga called to her daughter: "Look what I've brought home for supper!" And she dragged Tishka out of the sack. "Cook him well," she said to her daughter. "I'll be back soon."

Then she jumped onto her mortar and pestle and flew away.

Baba Yaga's daughter told Tishka to climb onto the spatula and sit quietly. Then she started to slide him into the oven.

But Tishka was too clever for her. He stretched and contorted his body so she could not fit him in.

"Sit still!" she shrieked. "Lower your head! Pull in your arms!"

"I don't know how," said Tishka. "Please show me."

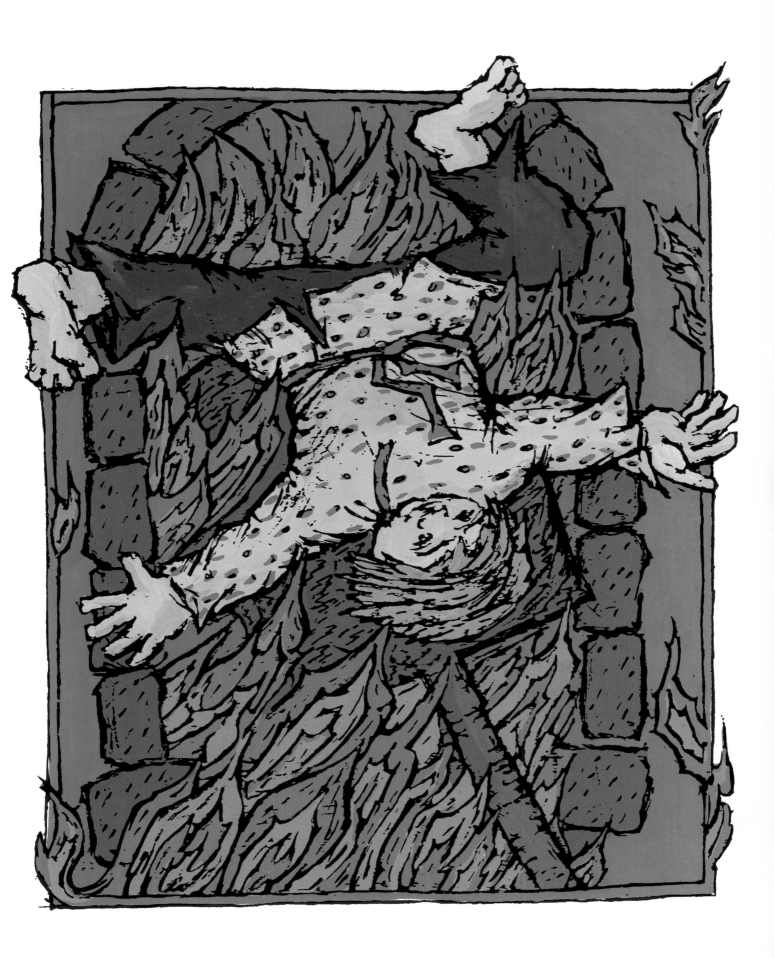

So the girl climbed onto the spatula and showed Tishka what she wanted him to do. She crouched down and drew up her knees so that she could easily fit through the oven doors.

Tishka instantly shoved her onto the hot coals and slammed the oven doors together. He jumped out of the front door of the house with chicken legs and climbed up a big old oak tree nearby. Just as he had hidden himself in the leaves, Baba Yaga appeared.

She flew down her chimney and began to eat, merrily humming after each bite. When she felt full and content, she strolled outside and rolled in the grass, singing: "Capturing Tishka was an easy feat. That poor little boy was good to eat."

From the top of the tree, Tishka called out: "Tricking your daughter was an easy feat. I'm glad you found her good to eat."

Baba Yaga looked up and spied Tishka in the oak tree. She turned bright green and stamped her feet, and the whole forest shook.

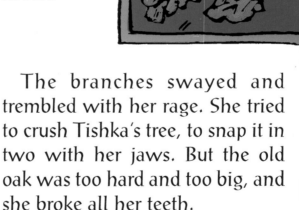

The branches swayed and trembled with her rage. She tried to crush Tishka's tree, to snap it in two with her jaws. But the old oak was too hard and too big, and she broke all her teeth.

So she ran to the blacksmith and had him forge her a new set of iron teeth. This time when she sank her teeth into the old oak tree, it started to crack and shake and split.

From the top of the tree, Tishka called out to a flock of geese: "Please, please, dear geese, spread your wings and fly me home."

But the geese answered: "Ga, ga, we're too tired. There's another flock of geese coming. Let them take you!"

Tishka looked down. Baba Yaga had almost gnawed through the trunk of the tree. One more bite and the tree would fall.

The other flock flew by, and Tishka called out: "Please, please, dear geese, spread your wings and fly me home. You'll get all the food you want."

But the geese answered: "Ga, ga, after us there is an ugly, hungry gosling. He'll take you."

By now the tree was teetering and about to crash. Baba Yaga grinned and licked her lips.

The ugly gosling flew by, and Tishka called out: "Please, please, dear goose, spread your wings and fly me home. You'll get all the food you want."

The ugly gosling took pity on Tishka and spread his wings for him. The tree fell just as they were flying away, leaving Baba Yaga with nothing but her fury.

When Tishka and the gosling arrived home, Tishka's parents were weeping: "Where! Where! Where is our son, our Tishka?"

And Tishka answered: "Here! Here! Here is your son, your Tishka!"

Tishka's parents embraced him, and their joy was endless. They could not stop kissing and hugging their son and his rescuer, the goose.

Tishka kept his promise to the gosling. He was given the best food and care and soon grew into a beautiful strong goose. He could fly faster and higher than any bird, so he became the leader of all geese.

Tishka and his parents lived happily ever after and were never bothered by Baba Yaga again.